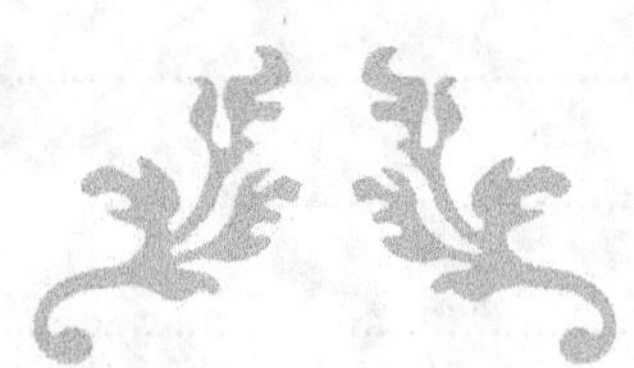

THE MIMICKER OF NATURE

Table of Contents

Chapter One: Uncertainty

One day while on a mission to Saturn's moon, the three astronauts saw a lot of space debris floating around in open space. The air was cold, and they were safe while inside of the pressurized and heated spaceship. Each astronaut was wearing a special top-secret suit from a secret lab underneath the Capital building.

WASA has explained to the public that they would have a few more missions to Saturn's moon. The tasks were carried out to see if there was a possibility of life on Saturn's moon.

Life on the earth keeps becoming scary with the passing days. As the earth gets older, many scary phenomenon's keep happening; these phenomenon's make one wonder and ask the question, "will there be a place for a man to run to if the earth becomes unsafe for one to live in"? This question had been crossing the minds of many. There are a lot of difficult issues happening

on the earth that will make us start considering a place of escape away from the earth. The ozone layer is said to be depleted due to human activities, which were believed to be targeted towards improving the standard of living of humans. In the bid to provide a better community and ensure the availability of employment, we humans had caused great damage to the ozone layer.

Time keeps ticking; as time goes on, the ozone layer becomes even more damaged than it used to be. As time goes on, the ozone layer may become so badly damaged that the earth may no longer be habitable for us humans. World leaders are doing all they can to minimize the damages caused to the ozone layer, but this still doesn't change the fact that humans continue to cause more and more damage to the ozone layer.

World leaders take every precaution to prevent the destruction of the ozone layer, just like delaying the inevitable. Once the layer gets destroyed, where do we go to? Where do we take cover from? This is a question that had been bothering most scientists. The ozone layer isn't the only issue to worry about. The air is filled with a lot of dangerous substances. Some of the things we do as we live our normal daily lives introduce pollutants into the air that we breathe. During the combustion of fuel, dangerous smoke is released into the air. When people smoke cigarettes, they introduce dangerous substances into the air.

When we practice open burning, we introduce dangerous substances into the air. All these substances introduced into the air continue to pile up and start causing harm to us. People start suffering from different lung diseases due to some pollutants that humans have released into the air.

Living our normal lives on earth and avoiding the release of these pollutants is challenging to avoid. Sometimes they are unavailable. This means that the earth will continue to be unsafe for human habitation.

With these in mind, scientists keep searching for alternatives; they keep searching for a safe place to avoid these dangerous pollutants. Whether this is possible or not, they keep trying; they aren't giving up because they know the dangers that man's activities are causing to man as man tries to survive on earth. Aside from the ozone layer being depleted and the air is polluted, something else has caused great worry over the centuries.

No matter how the world tries to be normal and live their daily lives as if everything is normal, they keep living in fear of being struck by this.

This thing is known as a pandemic. From generation to generation, the world keeps facing different forms of pandemics. No matter the precautions the world tries to take, no matter the measures the world put in place to the military against pandemics, it keeps hitting on them in different forms from time to time.

Whenever a pandemic hits the world, it often comes in the form of a certain disease that spreads faster than a wildfire. Most times, these diseases are airborne. Because they are airborne, they become straightforward to contract, and within a short period, many people start suffering from the particular disease. Most times, when these diseases strike, they often appear very strange and alien, in that there had never been a time in the past that they had been experienced. Because there had never been a time in the past when they had been experienced, scientists started struggling to know what the disease was all about.

It takes some time before they would be able to figure out what the disease is all about. After they had figured out what the disease was all about, they started looking for a cure or a vaccine. It normally takes a long time before they can find either a cure or a vaccine. Some of these diseases came into existence as a result of genetic mutation.

When a disease comes into existence due to genetic mutation, finding a cure becomes even more cumbersome. The scientists will continue to research possible cures. Still, before they start doing that, they would have tested other drugs or vaccines already in existence that seemed like they would have some effects on the disease if they can't prevent the disease; that is when the scientists will start working on their research. Sometimes it takes close to a year to be able to get a cure or a vaccine. This means that so many people will die before scientists come up with a cure or a vaccine.

While the scientists are carrying out their research, the government of every country will put different measures to help prevent this disease from spreading too fast and killing so many people. These measures could include physical distancing and a lockdown. Whichever measure the government of every country tries to put in place, the pandemic gives a tough blow to the world economy.

A lot of companies and businesses will go bankrupt. As a way to maintain their profit margin, they will start reduction of staff. So many people will become unemployed. There will be a lot of hunger everywhere. People will try to do anything possible to survive, and that includes crime. The rate of crime will surge very high because most countries will be struggling with recession. Many people will be battling with depression, and out of these people battling with depression. A pandemic is one of the scariest things that would ever hit the earth. Scientists knew this; this is why they keep working on finding an alternative, a place that's not the Earth where a man can survive.

Another thing that seems to be becoming a huge problem to the world right now is terrorism. Terrorism is gradually becoming the order of the day in most countries.

Once a terror group strikes, they cause a lot of damages to lives and properties; they cast the shadow of fear among people living around where the attack had been carried out. There are times when terrorists take a particular part of a country and turn it into their own. They establish their laws in this place they had captured and make life unbearable for those living there.

They bring developmental activities around this place that they had captured to a standstill. No one will want to migrate to this place under the rule of terrorists, and no one will like to establish a business around there. Those living there will continue to look for an opportunity to escape from there to somewhere else. The country's government that had a part or some parts of it under the rule of terrorists will have a lot of challenges to deal with.

They will spend a lot, and a lot of lives will be put on the line to eradicate these terrorists. Experience had shown that once terrorists were able to capture a particular place and turn it into their own, it becomes tough to eradicate them; even after they had been won, we see some little trace of their activities.

They are so difficult to be wiped completely because they hide among innocent civilians. The government will always consider these civilians' safety whenever they want to engage the terrorists in a fight.

The stress and the risks are too many to mention. Terrorists are known for gross human rights abuse; they deprived people of their rights and condemned people to death without any fair hearing. One alarming thing about terrorists is how they punish those living in the places they had captured, those they believe had gone against their rules.

They always punish them using capital punishment and kill them in the most gruesome way ever possible. Every country in the world is living in fear of being attacked by terrorists. Every government is on alert to prevent possible terror attacks. This is not an easy something to do.

Owing to this, there had always been needing to look for a place one can fall back to should the earth be under terror attacks; this is also why scientists keep searching for other planets that could be habitable.

Another thing we must not forget is that the Earth is getting old due to continuous usage. Humans have been on the Earth for millions of years, and we already know that most human activities are wearing down the Earth somehow.

Who knows, one day, the Earth may become tired from all these and start collapsing. Most houses that were built on earth, after very long years of experience at some point, start falling apart. A house built on earth can barely last three centuries.

If a house built on earth can barely last three centuries, how much more is the earth itself? The Earth has been in existence for thousands of centuries; there are a lot of changes that have happened on the Earth.

Just like an old house that keeps changing as it wears from old age, the Earth's most likely changing from wearing from old age. The Earth may collapse one day. When the Earth starts collapsing, humans will need somewhere safe to run to; this is also why searching for a habitable place is sacrosanct.

There are so many natural phenomenon's that have proven to be very detrimental to human existence over the years. These phenomenon's have, in most cases, made life very miserable and unbearable for man.

These phenomenon's are best regarded as natural disasters. We have always heard reports of how wildfire destroyed a lot of lives and properties.

Dying under the attack of fire is one of the most painful ways to die. When wildfire comes, it takes lives; it also takes properties. Apart from wildfire, we have earthquakes. Just like the wildfire, earthquakes had over centuries destroyed a lot of lives and properties.

People struggle and labor to make many investments; it takes them a lot of years to achieve these investments, sometimes it takes almost a lifetime of hard work to achieve these investments, but when wildfire and earthquake come, they destroy everything in a single day. All the struggles, labor, and energy people put into achieving everything just get wasted due to wildfire and earthquake in a single day.

Many people have been victims of this, and no one is to be blamed because they are natural disasters that happened independently. The most unlucky ones are those that got killed in the process. Apart from wildfires and earthquakes, we also have flooded.

 Floods have also caused a lot of loss of lives and properties. The only difference between flood and earthquake plus wildfire is that one can, to some extent, control the menace caused by flood by making suitable constructions.

Though people now make buildings that could withstand some magnitude of earthquakes, this is still not all that reliable because an earthquake is a natural disaster that we can't limit its extent.

We also have a volcanic eruption. The volcanic eruption had often proven very deadly and a master in the destruction of lives and properties. There are many other natural disasters, and they keep hitting different parts of the Earth whenever they choose to.

With the way natural disasters keep attacking the world and causing destruction to lives and properties, finding another habitable place free from natural disasters might look like a very wise proactive measure to take. This is also why scientists keep searching for an alternative place outside the earth that could be habitable to man.

The astronauts going to Saturn's moon were so nervous about the mission that some of them were shaking.

After a while, their nervousness left them, and they were ready to explore Saturn's moon. They found a way to get hold of their concern. This is one thing about making big moves in people's lives. When one wants to make big moves in life, there are nervousness and uncertainty that come in and try to hinder them from making that move.

This is mainly because they were trying to make a move for the first time, and they already knew that there were risks involved. People who can't take risks will most likely not achieve big things in life because there is always a risk involved for every big thing one wants to achieve.

The more significant the achievement, the bigger the chance one would have to face. Fear has always been why people avoid taking risks; this same fear has been the reason behind most failures people had been experiencing in life.

Courage had never for once been the absence of fear. Those people we had always celebrated all over the world as being very courageous didn't at some point had fear to execute that thing for which they are being observed to be bold.

Courage is when there's fear, but one still finds a way to push through even amidst the fear. Fear becomes so easy to overcome when you start seeing the encounter you are afraid of as something you are meant to do, as something you must do, no matter what. These astronauts were worried, but for the better good ahead, which they believe they must achieve, they found a way to build courage and go on the mission, which they had accepted because they thought it was the right course. They were now only orbiting Saturn's moon, and soon we're going to land on Saturn's moon. The inside of the cabin was still lovely and warm and cozy.

They felt too comfortable that they wished they wouldn't move any further. The astronauts were feeling kind of lazy and didn't want to move or even float around.

The astronauts weren't given any weapon or even a laser to protect themselves from what they might encounter, which made them nervous. They had managed to overcome the nervousness of undertaking the mission; now, they had another concern that seemed like it would remain with them until they were done with the task and safely returned to the Earth.

They didn't know what they were going to meet ahead of. The fear of the unknown is one of the worst fear one could ever encounter. When one is afraid of the unknown, everything around becomes a suspect. Once one hears a sound that might even be from their footsteps, they become excessively alert and scared; some people even become afraid of their own shadow. These astronauts were nervous about the unknown for some specific reasonable reasons.

Most of these planets had aliens living in them. Some of these aliens are rumored to come once in a while to spy on the Earth. They know about the existence of humans and, most times, see humans as threats to their existence.

This is because humans are brilliant. Humans keep discovering things. Humans keep expanding the horizon of their intelligence. This can be done in many ways, including going to other planets and making discoveries about them.

When humans now go to these planets to make discoveries, the aliens there see them as a nuisance trying to either exploit them or cause harm to them.

They know how humans will go the extra mile to look for making things easier and better for themselves. So, they might be believing that the humans would try to use them to their advantage. So, in a way to prevent humans from exploiting and taking advantage of them. It's natural for every territorial organism to try to protect the sovereignty of its territory.

Humans don't like aliens coming to the Earth because they believe aliens are spying on them and may undermine their sovereignty and safety. This is the same with aliens. These astronauts knew that once they encountered aliens, they would be in for a lot of trouble.

Aliens aren't the only thing to be afraid of out there. There could be other creatures that might be more dangerous than the aliens out there. They didn't know what these creatures would look like because they had never been there before.

At least aliens could operate under a particular order. They may get arrested and tortured to expose what their mission was all about when arrested by aliens; this would buy them more time for survival. But once a scary creature that's not an alien and could harm humans was involved, they may not even get the chance to say their last goodbye to each other. They had all these issues to worry about, yet they didn't have any weapon to protect themselves.

If they had some guns, they would have at least had little confidence. Apart from aliens and dangerous creatures, they had something else they should worry about, and it was something that weapons wouldn't be able to protect them from. This is the possibility of them being exposed to some sort of radiation. If they had sophisticated weapons, they wouldn't be able to protect them from radiation.

Even though they were dressed to protect them from being harmed by radiation, who knows if they would encounter radiation that would be stronger than whatever protective stuffs they were wearing to protect themselves. Those who sent them there didn't know everything was happening there; they might have perhaps not sent them on the mission if they knew.

Chapter Two: Preparation

They were given one flying and one ground-dwelling drone. These drones were worth millions of dollars and would help to survey the planet's surface. With these, they didn't need to go about a lot. They just needed to go about a bit enough to get the valuable information they were there for. The flying drone can fly over any landscape on any planet.

The flying drone can fly at a max speed of eighty-five miles per hour, and the drone that rolls on the ground can go at a top speed of fifty miles per hour. The drones are constantly on the move and don't need to slow down to take a break. They were all made to be very fitting for the mission; the astronauts didn't need to put in too much work to get them working very fine.

The astronauts were given plenty of space, food, and water. Usually, if they were expected to last three days on the mission, they would be given enough food and water that should last for six days or more. This is very necessary because no one knows how things would turn out over there; they had to prepare for unforeseen circumstances. They could become lost from each other and will have to take time before finding each other. This could happen when they encounter danger and start running from trouble.

So many other things could keep them away more than they were required to stay, but they were to do their best to return to the earth as quickly as possible. The less time it takes them to accomplish their mission and return to the world, the safer they become.

The three astronaut's names were Lucas, Gary, Linnet. Lucas is on the tall side and is always worried about his looks. He likes to be clean-shaven and loves to spend time working out.

He has large arms and has a left arm sleeve of tattoos. His tattoos were drawn that one standing five meters from him could see them. Gary's a quiet kind of guy and is known to be a loner. He loved being on his own and never enjoyed associating with people. He doesn't like to be around large crowds of people. Gary didn't enjoy meeting new people.

He angers very quickly, and this causes him to get into some disputes with other people. People who have anger issues rapidly get annoyed. At the slightest thing one does to them, they become pissed off; this makes them start acting somehow.

Gary knew he had anger issues; he didn't like people who make him angry and ruining his mood; this was why he had mastered the art of staying on his own and socializing less with people over the years.

This seemed to be one of the only ways to stay focused on whatever he was doing and avoid so many bad energies. Sometimes, he would be staying on his own, and people would come to him and just make him mad.

In as much as he couldn't do anything about this, he hated it so much. Linnet is a Mother and has two healthy children waiting for her at home. She loves her children very much and is always telling them how much she loves them. She had her kids when she was thirty-four years old and is now forty years old.

Her kids meant everything to her. Before she had her kids, she never knew that motherhood would be one of the sweetest things she had ever experienced. She had avoided being pregnant because she didn't want to go through the stress of being pregnant and caring for a child.

Pregnancy changes a woman in so many ways. It involves a lot of sacrifices. Once a woman becomes pregnant, her body starts changing in ways she may not be comfortable with. There might be some lifestyles she enjoyed so much before she became pregnant that may not be favorable to her pregnant state.

If she continues with this lifestyle, it would mean harming her baby, and maybe herself too. She enjoyed this lifestyle so much and didn't want to leave it, but she had to sacrifice this lifestyle that meant a lot to her because of her state. Then her body starts changing in ways she didn't like. She loses that banging body of hers which she believed has made so many people admire her. She's made to sleep in a position she isn't used to for the baby's safety.

She endures this state for nine whole months; after that, the time for delivery comes. She goes into labor. Labor pain is one of the most painful experiences someone would ever be exposed to; it cannot be described in words.

After going through the pains, the baby now comes. After the baby has been born, another series of work now sets in. There is this part of caring for a baby that's so consuming. This is the part that involves staying awake during the night.

The baby will often wake during the night and remain sharp for a long time; the mom will have to wake up to keep the baby from crying. After all the work involved in caring for the baby, the baby is now growing. Some other responsibilities now have set in.

The bills will start going high, and the mom will be so much involved in it, it becomes even more complicated if the mom is a single mom. Linnet knew all these, that was why she did all she could to avoid pregnancy at the early stages of her youth, but after she got her kids, she discovered how blessed she was. There was this special joy she always had whenever she remembered that she had kids that were at home waiting for her.

This extraordinary happiness she always found in her whenever she was around her kids and looking at them. Sometimes, the thought that she was the one that brought those lovely kids into the world overwhelmed her.

Whenever they called her 'mom,' it made her feel like she was on top of the world. There were times she would return home looking depressed or so worked out, the only thing she would be craving for at moments like this would hug from her beautiful kids, and they sure knew how to do it well. So now that she was on a mission, she couldn't get them off her mind.

She wondered if they had eaten, if there was anything they needed, if they were having any problems in school if they needed someone to help them with their homework, and many other kinds of stuff. They were all over her mind even as she had to focus on the mission she was on.

Her mother's watching over her children while she's on the space mission. Although she doesn't know how long she will be on this particular mission. She was told that the mission was going to be a four-year mission, This is the first mission that she has been on.

She knew that she might have to be away from her children for a while and was now okay with it. Initially, she didn't think she could pull it through. She didn't know she could ever be able to stay away from her kids, even for a single day.

It was very challenging for her. It wasn't an easy decision for her to make. She would be away from her kids for four years, and the most difficult part was that she wouldn't even be on the earth; she would be on another planet. She struggled with making up her mind, but it was working; after all, she had to do it, no matter what, since it was what she had signed for.

One of the things that gave her deep worry was how her kids would be cared for when she struggled to make up her mind; then, she remembered her mom. Her kids loved her mom so much, and they got along so well. She now figured out that her mom was the only one that could take good care of her kids while she was away.

She had her tied up, and today was feeling good and was ready to walk on Saturn's moon. She was hoping that nothing terrible was going to happen. She was told that there might be a good chance of meeting an alien species while checking out the moon.

She kept that thought in the back of her mind for the rest of the day. It was part of what she was afraid of about the mission, but she was already suppressing it. They weren't the first people ever going to space.

Most of those who went to space before or to other planets returned to the earth in one piece. Though there are a few cases where a few fatalities were recorded, it was somewhat minimal. The most considerable consolation she was having was that she wasn't going alone; she had companions going with her. Before they knew it, they were ready to land on the surface of Saturn's moon Titan.

The ground was very uneven, and the spacecraft how to take some extra time to keep itself self-balanced correctly. The craft slowly landed and was now settled down.

The three astronauts were soon ready to embark on their mission. The astronauts were all given a camera to film what they were doing while on the task. This will provide concert evidence or view of whatever they find intriguing that they encounter in their mission.

They were all given cameras and not just one person having a camera and the others just following along; they had different eyes and could spot things differently. They also had different ways of making judgments about things. Gary looked over and said into his microphone, is everyone ready to get out of this stinky sweaty spacecraft.

Linnet leaned over towards Gary, alright, let's go, everyone. The surface of the planet was very uneven, and there were many craters on the surface. There was some foliage growing up from the surface of the earth.

The plants kind of resembled the daisies that live on earth. There were a few huge boulders next to their spacecraft. The boulders were as giant as a house, there were some loose rocks around the large boulders. Everything seemed to be calm and quiet on the planet.

There wasn't much of an atmosphere, and you could see straight up into dark space. All of a sudden, the three astronauts heard a loud stomping sound. They looked all around the area and didn't see anything.

They were looking so frightened. They were getting into the planet and hadn't even lasted for a minute, and something strange was already happening. They were going to take their time to survey the vicinity around where they just landed, but the sound they had heard seemed to had taken all of their attention.

They were all focused on knowing what was making the sound or where the sound was coming from. It was an odd sound; it sounded like a stamp of Bulls. Gary looked ahead of them and saw that the ground had shifted. He was astonished about what he just saw.

They could have walked on the turned earth without knowing. Who knows, they might sink into the ground before they know it. He felt he had to alert others so that they would take all the necessary precautions necessary.

If the place was that way, there were possibilities that other places on the planet would be that way too. What it meant was that they had to look carefully before they leap.

"Hey, what?"

"I think I found out where all the noise is coming from."

Just one hundred yards in front of us, I saw that the ground was moving. Linnet couldn't understand what Gary meant. She couldn't understand what he meant by that the earth had shifted because it sounded like he was referring to an earthquake or a landslide. If that was true, how come they all didn't notice it when it happened.

"How so?"

"Gary could feel the surprise in her tone."

The ground just looked like it shifted its position. I don't think it's safe for us to walk over the shifting grounds. We might lose our balance and trip over it.

"What do you think?"

"We should do what we are supposed to do and not worry about the ground shifting."

Chapter Three: Socializing

Lucas didn't seem bothered about what Gary was saying; perhaps he didn't believe that the land was shifting or he didn't just look bothered. Lucas was all about starting whatever they came for as quickly as possible. Though they still had a lot of time to spend on the planet, there was no reason to rush.

He wasn't feeling like going about the whole place at the time; he wanted to start working with what he was already seeing.

I'm not in the mood for exploring today; let's get some dirt samples and find some plants that we can put in test tubes. If it's okay with everyone, I will stay here and do what I'm supposed to do while you two explore. Remember to be careful and don't get lost.

They were warned so many times about getting lost before they went into the mission. The planet wasn't small, and they didn't know their ways around since it wasn't a place they were conversant with. Staying together and doing stuff together was their possible way of avoiding getting lost.

It was also their possible way of surviving from whatever potential danger that they may encounter. Like for example, they just met the ground shifting. Linnet and Lucas couldn't find where the sound was coming from or what was bringing about the sound, but Gary was able to discover what the sound they had heard was all about and had alerted them of the possible danger ahead.

If they weren't together, maybe Lucas and Linnet wouldn't have noticed that the ground was shifting. We won't, now don't worry about us. I won't work then. Make sure that Gary doesn't do anything stupid, or I will report it back to WASA. Gary had always been the kind of person that loved doing crazy things.

He was the kind of person that never takes enough precautions when doing something; he could be reckless sometimes. They all knew his personality, and if they didn't watch out, he could land them into some trouble. He was the kind of person that always found it challenging to stay out of trouble. They were mainly told to keep on the lookout for him. I can see some rocks floating in midair; I wish I could swim in the air as those rocks do. I wonder what's making those rocks float above us. Gary said as he seemed intrigued by the sight of the floating rocks.

They didn't look reasonably possible, but they were possible because they weren't on the Earth. The Earth has a gravitational force that would never allow anything to float on the air once thrown up.

A rock thrown up in the planet will most likely start falling back after it has attained its maximum possible height, which would most likely be limited by gravity and some air the rich will be encountering as it projected high. It wasn't that way in this planet they were in, and its sight looked astonishing.

The rocks weren't all small, some of them were big, but they looked like they would fall. Those big rocks were so big that they could even kill someone if they eventually fell down on someone's head.

Those rocks look like big rocks and would probably injure one of us. Just don't stand beneath one, Linnet said as she tried to warn Gary. She was already seeing the curious and adventurous looks in his eyes and had to remind him about the risk involved if he tried doing anything funny around the rocks.

I want to see, Gary said. He was now sounding like a stubborn child that was refusing to listen to the counsel from the elders. Linnet was now looking a bit angry; she couldn't understand how a grown man would be acting as if he was still a kid. Alright, go ahead and stand underneath the one floating rock. I feel like I'm babysitting my kid with you.

"How so?"

"I have to tell you what to do and what not to do."

Gary didn't like someone telling him what to do. He was the kind of person that didn't want to be treated as if he didn't know what he was doing. He was now feeling like Linnet was trying to tell him what to do, and he wasn't feeling okay about it. No, you don't, I'm my own man, and I do what it is I want to. Gary yelled, he was already getting heated up, but Linnet wasn't looking like she would get loose of him.

You don't think about what could happen if one of those rocks fell on top of you. I'm just amazed at how the rocks float. Gary was already displaying what he was known for.

If he were left unchecked, he would most likely do something that would either harm him or all of them. If it were possible, they would prefer to do whatever they came for quietly and leave without any potential threats out there, noticing their presence on the planet.

Still, with Gary around, his attitude may get things ruined for them if they don't put him under check. Now, remember, Gary, we can only be out here for four hours, then we need to get back into the spacecraft to refill our oxygen tanks in our spacesuits.

I don't want to tell your mom that you died on my watch, Gary. Gary was now feeling uncomfortable with working with Linnet. He now thought that she was now unnecessarily too emotional. He didn't want to sound or look sexist, but he was now seeing it as if her woman nature was taking a significant toll on her. He would have preferred it if he was going with Lucas or even alone. He didn't have the strength to start wasting his time arguing over something.

The mission might be scary; it might be something he wouldn't have loved getting involved with if it wasn't for work sake, but he was there already; since he was already there, he had to do all he could to exploit everything he could lay his eyes on that caught his interest. He didn't want someone cautioning him; he believed he knew what was dangerous when he saw one.

Gary was now thinking that splitting from Linnet and working separately might be his only option. He knew she would try to throw some tantrums, but he would do his best to cut loose from her. Why don't you and I split up and survey the area for a few miles? Gary suggested. Linnet already knew what he was thinking; she knew he wanted some freedom to practice his mischievousness without anyone being around to caution him.

He might end getting himself killed or even get all of them killed. She was never going to let that happen. Before they left the earth, they were always instructed to tag along together and prevent getting lost. Splitting at that moment when they didn't even know they were gone from their right on the planet was a terrible idea.

Also, they were clearly warned about Gary's attitude. Everyone knew him and what he was capable of. It was as if their superiors knew he would start acting up and asked them to always be on the lookout for him. Linnet decided that she wasn't going to split from Gary. There were times his head would seem to be cool, and he would be acting like a very reasonable person.

There were times he would start putting out his stubborn attitudes, Linnet believed he was currently putting out his crazy perspective, and she would remain around him to save him from himself. No, we aren't going to split up, especially out here. Linnet said in a solid tone to show Gary how determined she was about remaining by his side. She could see frustration building all over Gary. Come on, Gary said in frustration.

From the looks on Gary's face and his body composure, if Linnet were the type to be easily swayed, she would have let him have his way.

He wasn't thinking in his best self for her to let him have his way. The answer is no, so just get over it. Linnet responded in a voice that sounded firmer than the last time.

At this point, it downed on Gary that he couldn't have his way. Linnet wasn't looking like she was going to give him the freedom he was asking for;

he now mellowed down and brought back his team spirit from where he had kept it. If an evil spirit exists, then maybe he was possessed by one, and the evil spirit that had possessed him seemed to have just left him.

Aside from Gary's crazy attitude, which he displayed sometimes, he was an enjoyable person to be with and was always very dedicated to his job. This must have been why he was selected for the mission.

Despite what seemed like his shortcomings, he was good at noticing things quicker than others, and he was good at providing results. They started exploring; there were no more arguments. Now I'm done exploring the floating rocks; let's check out the area with foliage around it.

These plants look so strange; this plant off to the left of you, Linnet, reminds me of a Venus flytrap. It does, but it's different than plants that grow on earth. Watch out, there's a long green vine that's crawling towards your left leg.

I've never seen a vine be able to crawl along, I think that you better move away from that green vine. I don't think that green vine likes you.

"Where should I stand then?"

"You should stand by me over here and leave that green vine alone."

As Gary walked towards Linnet, the green vine stopped crawling after him. See that, you got too close to the green vine. Now, Gary seemed to be in his thoughts; he seemed to be wondering about something. He then looked around them for a concise while and took his gaze back to Linnet, who didn't notice that Gary seemed to be wondering about something.

How comes we haven't seen any other life forms besides plants? Gary asked. Since they went to the planet, he observed that the only living creatures they saw were just plants. They had told them they should be mindful of aliens, but he had yet to see any evidence of aliens or other creatures aside from plants.

Not like he wanted to encounter aliens, at least not now that they haven't even been that long on the planet, but he wondered if plants were the only creatures that could survive on the earth. That's a good question; I don't know. Linnet responded. She hadn't really thought about it, but immediately Gary asked the question, she realized that they saw plants, no other living thing on sight.

You know, I'm surprised that Lucas didn't want to come with us. He couldn't understand why Lucas decided to stay behind while they went for the survey. He didn't think about it then when Lucas said he was going to stay behind. Now that he was thinking about it, it felt like Lucas was bossing them around.

"How's your oxygen supply?"

"It shows that it's still at one hundred percent."

Their oxygen was like one of the most things that mattered most to them. Any issue with their oxygen supply could lead to their death.

Mine shows the same; that's a good thing our oxygen is still good. Gary was now wondering what could be below the ground that they were standing on. On the Earth, they had water below the ground. There were also rocks below the ground, and there were some places where one could go and find some minerals below the ground.

These minerals are mainly seen as natural resources and could provide revenue to whoever the country wants to harness them.

"What do you think is below the bottom of this planet?"

"Probably boring old dirt"

Gary had been noticing some strange dispositions from Linnet. He had known her for a very long time and could guess when she wasn't feeling okay. She was the kind of person that smiled a lot and laughed a lot. She was always cheerful, she had this straightforward way of bringing humor to work.

Sometimes she would tell funny stories about her kids while they worked, and they would all laugh about it; she didn't seem to be flowing well with what they were doing. Gary seemed not to have noticed her cheerfulness since they got into the planet. He knew she wasn't feeling herself. You don't seem very excited about this mission, Linnet.

Gary said in a tone that looked more prying than sympathetic. No, I'm getting bored of it and wish I could be alone and not with anyone else. Linnet's mood was very understandable.

She was a mom that had left her lovely kids on earth and had gone to another planet. She was exposed to certain dangers which she didn't even know their nature or where they were hiding and waiting for her. She could die from the mission, and when that happens, she would never see her beautiful kids again. They would miss her a lot.

Chapter Four: Passing Time

She knew her mom would do her very best to care for them, but the truth was that they would forget that very motherly love which only her could give to them.

She missed their smiles and how they laughed with her. She kept yearning to embrace them into her arms. She knew that nothing could match the feeling she always felt whenever she held her kids in her arms, but now she was just out there on a lonely planet and feeling bored about everything.

She had been struggling to hide what she was feeling, but even in Gary's weaknesses, he was so good at observing things, he had been able to keep what she had been trying so hard to hide under her sleeves.

"Why's that?"

"I'm thinking about my kids and other stuff."

Linnet said in a manner that conveyed how subdued she was. Gary could feel her pains. He knew how much she loved her kids and how difficult it was for her to make up her mind to join in the mission.

Mainly because she didn't want to leave her kids behind. He was now feeling very sorry for her and was wishing if there was anything he could do to make her feel better, at least for the moment.

He could remember most of the arguments he always had with her resulted from him trying to do crazy things that could harm him. She would disagree with him and refuse to allow him to have his way.

She could be very annoying at those times, and he would even regret ever knowing her during those times, but after everything, he knew it was her way of looking out for him to make sure he didn't do things that would harm him. To him, they have worked a long time enough and have had enough experiences together that he couldn't just see her as a work partner. She was also like a friend to him.

I'm sure I could do something silly to cheer you up. There's no time to cheer me up; let's continue walking towards these tall plants. So Linnet thought that the faster they got into what they came for, the faster they would get done with it; this would determine how quickly they would get home.

For her, if they could finish quick enough, maybe they could return earlier than proposed, and she could meet her lovely kids again.

There were tall plants before them. Gary looks amazed as it seems like he is just sighting them for the first time.

The plants looked tall, taller than what we usually see on earth; this caught Gary's attention that he had to fix his gaze on them for a moment.

Wow, this plant must be over eight feet tall, and this plant next to it is just four feet tall. You sound like you are good with measuring stuff; yes, I am.

"What else do you want me to count?"

"Why don't you measure how tall this plant is next to me?"

"That plant's hard to measure."

If I had to guess, I would say that it's seven feet tall. Hey Linnet, Yes.

"Could we sleep outside of the craft?"

"No," you can't

We still haven't contacted the alien life supposed to live on this planet. There's supposed to be alien life on this planet. Linnet was kind of surprised by this question that Gary just asked.

Wasn't he listening when they were briefed about the earth even before they started their mission? Or was he just acting dumb? On second thought, she realized that Gary sometimes never listens when listening does matter. Yes, there is I'm getting excited now.

> "How many different kinds of alien life forms are supposed to be living on this planet?"

> "There are supposed to be two."

Just remembering that there are likely two other forms of aliens that are supposed to be living on the earth, they sent chills all over Linnet.

> "What if these aliens now came together to attack them?"

> "Usually, when aliens of different species live together, there's a lot of likelihood of them fighting each other."

Prevalent things might sometimes be the reason behind them fighting each other, whatever or however big the reasons for which they are fighting are; they are still intelligent, they could decide to form an alliance and bring their forces together to fight a common enemy whom they believe is a threat to their existence.

"What are they called?"

"WASA didn't say."

"Can I make up a name for the alien creatures?"

"Yes," you can

Call them whatever you want to. Just that moment, Gary's sight caught something that looked like a tree. It was the first time he saw a tree on the planet; he then walked closer to it as he seemed astonished by the features he was observing about the tree or whatever it was. Gary was touching it and was feeling the texture of what he felt was a tree.

They were warned about touching plants; they were told to be very careful, at least they shouldn't connect with their bare hands, but Gary seemed to have either forgotten this, or he was just careless. After all, he didn't like someone telling him what to do.

Hey, look what I'm standing next to; it seems like a tree; it's the first one I've seen. Linnet was surprised by the way Gary was touching the tree. The tree could be poisonous to humans. Some plants are believed to be toxic to humans; humans do their best to keep these plants as far as possible from themselves.

These plants don't even grow close to where humans are staying. Even when adults can avoid having contact with these plants, kids could still get in touch with these plants without knowing that these plants could be harmful to them.

That was the Earth, they live in the world, and they knew their ways around there and knew how to take safety precautions from such plants. But now they were on a strange planet, and they had been warned to be very careful, even with plans, but Gary is too carefree. You really should not be touching the alien plant life.

Linnet complained as she tried to caution him. I think it's safe to feel, Gary responded in a very carefree tone. No, it's not.

"Would you please get away from that tree?"

"Linnet said immediately."

Apart from the tree being poisonous, it could also be used as a trap against them. They had to be very wise in whatever they were doing on the planet and always consider the worst thing that could ever happen; this might be their only way of returning to the earth in one piece.

Gary was now seeing Linnet as someone very dull to work with. He didn't like the fact that she was too cautious. Gary had always maintained that people who act too cautiously end up making huge mistakes in life.

He believes that those who try so hard to avoid making mistakes are the ones that end up making the most mistakes. You are just no fun, Gary said to her in a subdued tone. I know that, but it's my fault if you get hurt.

Now please think before you do something stupid. But please come over here with me and take a look at these rows of trees. Linnet didn't see what Gary saw as a tree to be a tree. Gary was a scientist; she couldn't understand why he was always so dumb. Sometimes she would be wondering if he went to college. Even high school students could sometimes make better judgments than Gary.

He was quick at sighting things and was good at getting results, but sometimes his dumbness makes one wonder if he was the one with all the good qualities he was known for. They aren't trees.

"How many times am I going to have to tell you?"

"Just twice, that's what I thought."

This alien tree has strange markings on it. Okay, enough with the exotic trees, let's get moving on. Linnet was now looking ahead; something seemed to have caught her attention.

She had to stop walking to take a clear look; it was a cave. Hey, look, Gary, there's a large cave a few feet away from us. Gary now sighted to see the cave. Now that Linnet was looking at the shelter, the thought that there could be a creature living in there now came to mind.

Over there on the Earth, a lot of life discoveries had been made from caves. Caves had often helped make a lot of findings of stuff that happened in the past, probably during the primitive era. Whenever scientists were on an exploration mission, they permanently attached a lot of importance to caves.

The biggest problem with going into strange caves is that dangerous creatures could be living there. For some reason, Linnet seemed not to think about the threat in the cave ahead of them. She saw it as an opportunity for them to make huge findings within a minimal amount of time.

She believed that there would be stuff that would quicken what they came for, and the quicker they were done with what they came for, the better for her because she would be returning earlier enough to meet her kids.

"What do you think lives in the cave?"

"Probably an alien chicken, Gary said."

Linnet felt Gary was making a joke about the situation, and she wasn't happy about it. The cave before them was an important finding that needed their seriousness. No, there's no time for jokes up here. Now think for a moment and give me the correct answer.

Gary now looked at her; he could see that she meant business this time. He thought briefly then looked at her; Probably a large alien creature, okay, that sounds better than a foreign chicken.

Now were going to enter the cave. I don't want to go into the cave.

"Why not?"

"I'm scared that we are going to get lost in the cave and run out of oxygen."

Running out of oxygen was also something they were so frightened about. To avoid running out of oxygen, they would need to be close to their craft or be able to return to their craft before they run out of oxygen so they could refill their oxygen supply.

Linnet was at least relieved that Gary wasn't that much bothered about aliens at the moment. They could avoid getting lost if they didn't go too far and if they remained together.

This was another reason Linnet had insisted that they shouldn't split from each other. If one of them couldn't recognize the road or directions through which they had walked, the other could identify them, and this will reduce their chances of being lost.

No, we aren't going to get lost in the cave. Come on, now am I going to have to take you by the hand and force you to come with me or are you going to do it on your own. It would help if you didn't hold my hand, then let's go into the cave.

They both started walking towards the cave, with Linnet being ahead while Gary followed behind her, Linnet always stopped from time to time to look behind her to see if Gary was coming along. He didn't change his mind; he kept following her.

They both stepped into the cave. The cave was dark and felt cold. There was total silence in the cave. They had to be careful as they entered to avoid making too much sound.

"Do you think any animals are living here?"

"Yes," I do

I hope that animals are friendly and won't attack us.

"What if there is an alien waiting for us?"

"Now don't be silly"

There are no aliens here, and any aliens won't attack us. Linnet knew that Gary's question was valid. The thought of being shot in the cave was one of the fears she was battling with, but she had to struggle and suppress it so that Gary wouldn't notice a thing about it.

Chapter Five: Exploring

Before they decided to embark on the mission, they already knew that there were a lot of threats before them; they knew that some creatures on the planet might not like being graced with their presence.

On the Earth, there were are animals that are so unfriendly to man; whenever they see humans, they see humans as food that could satisfy their hunger. There were possibilities that there could be wild animals on this strange planet, probably in the cave, these wild animals may not be the type on the earth, but they could see them as food to satisfy their hunger.

Whichever it was against them, they were already on their mission; they were already in the cave too; they would face it. The best they could do was to run away since they had no weapon with them.

It had been made clear to them that they weren't going there to change anything on the planet; they weren't going there to go and carry out a war. It was believed the Earth was a natural habitat to some organisms, and it made no sense to go and start attacking them.

After all, they were scientists and not soldiers. Just get those thoughts out of your mind. I'm not happy to be in here either, Gary. Now they are standing at a spot with two pathways before them. One was to the left, and the other was to the right. They seemed to be bothered on which way to go as they looked from left to right. Okay, Linnet, we can either go to the right or left;

"Which way should we go?"

"Let's go to the right, oh, but I want to go to the left."

We aren't going to split up, so don't even think about it, Gary. I wasn't, yes you were. Linnet was even surprised that Gary was still harboring the thoughts of splitting from her even when they were inside a lonely cave with possible threats to their lives ahead. She had to retake a look at him to make sure he was really in his right state of mind or if he was joking.

Now, she wasn't just concerned about his safety; she was also worried about her safety. Walking alone in the cave with no man around here would be a foolish thing for her to do. She was pretty much afraid but had to be acting strong because Gary was around.

There was no way she was going to allow his split from her, at least not now. At times like this, there is a high possibility that one could get lost; even when one doesn't get lost, one may also need some help from a colleague.

There's a high possibility of one falling from a great height Into what might look like a pit in a cave. If they were together and one of them was to fall, the other would help rescue the other.

If one were to get injured in the cave, the other person would help take the wounded to safety. Some injuries may happen in a cave that might affect one so severely that one may not walk. In situations like this, the other colleagues or colleagues would have to help out.

There are a lot of advantages to going into a cave with someone than going alone, especially when you are going into the shelter for the first time and you don't even know your way around. They had now gone right and were quiet as they looked around the see what was around and ahead of them.

Gary said we should have gone to the left as he broke the silence between them for a few minutes. He felt like he was being controlled, but he didn't want to say anything about it, so they didn't end up arguing in the cave; it wasn't safe for them to start discussing when they should be looking out for each other. And tell me why you are thinking that way.

Linnet demanded almost immediately. She couldn't see anything wrong with her decision to move right and couldn't understand why Gary complained about it. Even after a short while, they left where the space split into two roads. Maybe if we had gone to the left, it would have been a more straightforward way than off to the right. Gary explained.

It sounded like one of the dumbest things Linnet had ever heard. It felt like he was trying to justify his decision to move left by all means. In most adventure movies, Linnet had been watching while she was on the earth; whenever one was hunting for a treasure or one was going to rescue someone, this person undertaking this adventure in the movie came across where roads were split into left-right. The road by the right had always proven to be the right road. Linnet had thought about this before insisting they followed the road to the right. After all, they were on a mission that was more or less like an adventure.

No, I'm afraid I have to disagree with you, Gary. Besides that, Gary, we both have two hours to get out of here and get back to our spacecraft before our oxygen runs out.

Linnet couldn't believe they just had two hours. This meant that they had to be fast with whatever they were doing in the cave and make sure they didn't go too deep into the cave.

Above all, they had to make sure that they didn't get lost in the cave. Whatever would keep them longer than they should be something they must do all they could to avoid.

I'm getting all itchy and sweaty and am tired of wearing this heavy spacesuit. You have to keep the spacesuit on, or you will die; it's just that easy. I understand that, so stop complaining about being all sweaty. I'm all sweaty, too, and you don't hear me complaining. Gary had always been a slow Walker. He was never the type one would love to walk with if one was running out of time on something; perhaps this was why he was so good at seeing things before others saw them.

Linnet was now feeling bothered about the way he was walking. If they should continue that way, they would most likely run out of time. He was walking so slowly, and he wasted time looking at things that didn't matter.

Now Gary looks straight ahead and keeps on walking, or I will knock you into next week. You walk like an older man, and you take forever. Alright, well,

> "What would you like me to do?"

> "I would like you to walk at a faster pace and keep up with me."

As they continued to walk, the interior of the cave ahead of them continued to get darker. Gary was beginning to worry about how dark the cave was becoming as they walked deeper. You know it's getting dark in here Linnet, I'm getting nervous. Linnet didn't seem bothered about the darkness they were entering into; she seemed to have a remedy for it and was even surprised that Gary had been walking into the night without thinking about any possible source of light for them; it took him time to start complaining.

"Do you have a flashlight with you?"

"Yes," I have it right here, Linnet responded.

Gary was now wondering why she didn't put on the light, and they had been struggling to see clearly in the cave.

"How come you didn't turn on the flashlight yet?"

"These space flashlights batteries don't last to save their artillery, but an hour then they need to be recharged again."

"Did you realize that?"

"No," I didn't know that about the space flashlight.

I have had enough of arguing with you, Linnet. Okay, Gary, then you need to agree with me more often on things. Then we won't get into a heated discussion. Linnet switched on her flashlight. That is a bright flashlight, Linnet. Yes, and be glad that it's so brilliant. Immediately, Gary stopped walking as he seemed to have heard something. Linnet was still walking without noticing that Gary had stopped walking; she had always been ahead since he wasn't all that fast in movement. Stop a minute, Gary said as he touched Linnet. Linnet couldn't understand why he was telling her to stop, but she knew that there must be something to it. Why? Linnet asked as she fixed her gaze on Gary, who seemed to be listening attentively to be sure of what he was hearing. I heard something.

"What is it that you heard?"

"It sounded like someone else was talking."

It sounded like another astronaut. I know it could not be another astronaut. Linnet said. She wasn't disproving whatever Gary had heard because she knew hearing and seeing things first were his specialty, but she didn't believe that another astronaut was with them or in the cave with them.

Lucas had stayed behind around where their spacecraft landed, and she was sure that he wasn't following them as they walked and explored things around them.

You never know, though, Linnet, stranger things have happened. Now I hear footsteps, and they sound like they keep on getting closer.

I think that we are going to find out soon enough what exactly it is. Linnet was now hearing the footsteps too. If they were astronauts like them, then they might be from another country.

This won't be much of an issue; they would have more people to work with and share their ideas. It will also mean more hands being put together whenever there is a life-threatening incident.

The biggest fear should be if the footsteps were from aliens or dangerous creatures that may want to harm them. Yes, that's right, Gary. I bet you that it's an alien species that is just trying to fool around with us.

That's a good guess, Gary, but aliens are far too intelligent to want to fool us. They probably already have us figured out. Just that moment, Gary started looking at the ceiling of the cave. He became even more worried than he was.

The top of this cave is not very high, Linnet. I hope that there is not an earthquake while we are here. No such thing will happen, Gary; I am just concerned that what we will come up against will be hostile and violent. No please don't say that, Linnet; you are manifesting for something to go wrong.

"Now you are trying to use big words on me, Gary?"

"Yes," I am

I won't speak if you think what I'm saying will worsen the situation.

"No," I don't mean that Linnet,

"Did what I say go entirely over your head?"

"It did."

Here it comes. Linnet could now see what had been approaching them. It must have heard them talking from where it was and decided to trace where they were in the cave.

"What is it?"

"It's a creature."

It's beginning to approach us. Gary had now sighted the beast, and he seemed to be trying to figure out what it was.

"Do you see him, Gary?"

"Yes," I do.

He reminds me of an alien gray; I hope that he won't hurt us. He has some massive eyes, though, and they are all black and are in the shape of an almond. Linnet was now looking afraid; she was now shaking as she talked. I can barely make out what his hands look like. He was a small slit for a mouth.

The creature seemed to have seen them now. It fixed its gaze on them as if it was kind of trying to make out what they were.

Perhaps it was seeing creatures like them for the first time, unless if some astronauts had visited the cave before them, but that didn't seem to be possible. Look, Gary; he's now looking directly at us. I'm so scared.

"Are you going to protect me?"

"Yes," I will.

Gary now sounded so manly.

"How about if I step right in front of you?"

"That sounds good to me."

I can't see a thing

"What's the creature doing now?"

"He's still walking forward towards us."

He doesn't seem like he has any expressions at all on his face. His face is all gray, just like the rest of his body. He has hands that are little and resemble an indicator of a child.

"How many fingers does he have?"

"He has six fingers and no nails."

There are no hairs on any part of his body. He has long legs that are so skinny that they resemble toothpicks.

“What's he doing now?”

“He's putting his right hand out and staring into my eyes.”

I will come out from in back of you, Gary and see what's going on. Linnet had been hiding behind Gary as she was talking. She now started looking at the creature again as she got a bit beside him. The beast was looking harmless to her. She was now feeling somewhat relaxed as she watched the creature approaching them.

Oh my lord, I've never met an alien life form before. this is so very exciting. Linnet, stop moving;

“Why?”

“The creature is now just ten feet away from me, and I don't want him to get startled, grab me or bite me. “

However, I don't think that this creature has any teeth. That creature looks very wimpy to me.

“What do you think?”

"No," the creature doesn't seem wimpy.

You didn't explain why to me; who cares about why. I don't know what kind of powers this alien may hold.

"Why don't you turn off your space flashlight?"

"Why it's not hurting anything. It may upset the alien, and he could attack us."

He hasn't attacked us yet, and I don't believe he wants to hurt us. He lives on this planet, and we are the ones who are invading his world.

"Why don't you try to speak to the alien?"

"I suppose that I could, just see if he says anything to you."

"Hi alien creature, how are you?"

"There was dead silence"

I don't think the alien wanted to hold any conversation with us. I believe that the alien creature wants to remain quiet.

74

All of a sudden, the alien kneeled and looked right at Linnet. I think that he likes you. No, he doesn't. Now stop trying to joke around with me. Gary, you cannot make jokes up here, and I wouldn't say I like your jokes anyway.

Suddenly the alien looked off to his left at the large open area of the cave. Gary and Linnet couldn't understand why the creature was looking in that direction. They looked properly but could see nothing.

"What do you think he is seeing?"

"I wouldn't know"

"What do you think?"

"Perhaps another alien creature, has arrived."

No, I don't believe that Linnet; maybe a giant creature is coming, and the little alien is scared of it. Now you are turning negative on me, Gary. I hope you are wrong. The creature looked somewhat frightened as it was still looking in the direction. Linnet seemed to have understood that the animal was afraid, but she couldn't understand why the beast was scared because she wasn't seeing any form of threat coming from where the beast was looking.

Then came a giant creature that resembled a vast chameleon. The creature's body was all gray but had orange stripes going down its entire back. Then he opened his mouth, and you could see were small pointy teeth with jagged edges.

He let out his tongue, and his tail began to sway back and forth. Linnet and Gary look frightened. Linnet mainly had found out why the little creature was scared. This giant creature looked like it was going to eat anything that stood in its way.

Chapter Six: Tight Spot

There was something about this huge creature that just caught Linnet's eyes. It had three eyes.

This was the first time Linnet was coming across an animal that had three eyes.

She didn't know if she was to categorize it as a reptile or something else. Snakes usually have just two eyes, but this one had three.

Look, Gary, this creature has three eyes instead of just two. That means that he can see us much better, don't say that

"What if I don't want him to see us?"

"He's right here already, Gary, and I bet he saw you while he was walking into here."

That's true, Linnet; I don't know why I'm so afraid of the creature; I guess I'm so scared of it, just because of how large the beast is. Just that moment, Linnet looked towards the spot the tiny creature had been standing; she couldn't find it anymore. She had noticed that it was afraid; the beast must have run for safety to avoid been eaten by this giant monstrous creature.

Pay attention Gary, look, the alien is gone.

"Did you see where he went?"

"No," I didn't

I was too focused on the giant creature. You made a big mistake by not watching where the alien had gone.

"What would you like me to do now?"

"Just stay here, and let's see what this giant creature decides to do."

"Why do you think that the alien ran away?"

"He was probably scared of the giant creature and hid somewhere.

Okay, since it's my fault for not watching the alien, should I look for him by myself. No, stay here with me. The giant creature had walked some footsteps closer to them and stopped. The creature seemed very aggressive, the looks on its eyes showed it was ready to cause harm, but it stopped as it seemed to be sensing something that Gary and Linnet were yet to notice. That giant creature is now twenty feet away from us and has stopped moving. I wonder why he stopped moving.

Look, his tail keeps on moving in a back and forth movement. The creature slipped his tongue back into his mouth. It looked like it had changed its mind towards advancing any further.

The beast let out a roar and began to retreat to where he came from. That was a scary encounter no, it wasn't so bad. I mean, the creature could have tried to stomp on us and kill us.

"Would you please let me look for the alien?"

"I don't want us to get separated."

Then if you get hurt, my neck will be on the line for allowing you to go on an adventure on your own. Suddenly, the ground began to shake; oh no, Gary, it's an earthquake.

We need to get out of this cave before it collapses. It now became clear why the creature had decided to go back. It sensed that something was about to happen; that was why it had to flee for safety and maybe take cover from where it believed it was safe. Just that moment, the little creature that had earlier gone missing came into sight again. Gary sighted the tiny creature as it remained standing and looking at them. Gary could figure out that the little creature was pretty much very confused.

Look, there's the alien; he's standing by the entrance of the cave. That's a good observation, Gary. Rocks were now falling from the ceiling of the cave into the spaces in the cave.

Watch out for the falling stones, Linnet; we need to go now, Gary; ouch, a rock just came down on my left foot. I dropped my flashlight, and it went rolling down the slight incline and is at the back of the cave.

We don't have the time to go back to get the flashlight. I didn't want to leave anything behind. Don't worry about it, our lives are more important than a flashlight.

Come on, hold onto me; then the ground began to shake once more. I can't keep my balance; could you please hold onto my right hand.

Yes, I will; it's hard to walk over such uneven surfaces. Hold on, Gary, I just fell, let me get up. You almost pulled me down with you. I know, and I'm sorry for that. We are almost out of here, I know. but

"Are we going to make it?"

"Yes," we will make it; the alien is still by the entrance of the cave.

Just a few more steps, and we will be home free. Gary and Linnet continued struggling. They made their way to the entrance of the cave and eventually escaped from the cave.

They now ran to give some space from the shelter so that rocks from its ruins wouldn't end up harming them. At last, we are finally out of the cave; now you understand why I said it was not a good idea to explore the cave in the first place.

You were right all along, I should have listened to you. Suddenly a few big rocks fell in front of the entrance of the cave. Gary wasn't all that wrong after all.

He was never in support of them going into the cave. Linnet didn't listen to him earlier because of his questionable personality. If it were Lucas that had suggested they shouldn't go into the cave earlier, she would have listened to him. Gary could now hear a roar that appeared to be from the giant creature that had three eyes. Despite all the rocks that had fallen into the cave, the beast was still very much alive and was even sounding more aggressive than it said before. Perhaps the fallen rocks had made it angrier and deadlier.

I think our lizard friend is getting angry because I just heard a roar. Suddenly, the top of the cave exploded open, and the giant creature came up out of the cave. Gary and Linnet could see what was happening, and it looked frightening.

The ground beneath them was so dry that it was beginning to crack. We need to get further away from here, Linnet. But I am worried that the giant creature will see us and try to chase after us.

No, the creature isn't even headed our way; he is currently run in the opposite direction of us. He moves at a slow pace, and if we have to, we could outrun him. But I want to take another look at the giant creature.

"Are you crazy?"

"No," but I've never seen such a fantastic-looking creature.

"Do you still see the alien?"

"Yes," he's standing by a tree

"Is he looking at us?"

"No," he minds his own business.

We need to study his behavior. We are already studying his behavior.

"What more do you want to know about the alien?"

"I want to find out what he eats."

I haven't seen many living organisms so far. I also would like to know what he prefers to drink. I don't think that he's going to tell us. If he doesn't speak to me, he won't talk to you either,

"I thought you said he likes me?"

"I did, but I was joking around with you."

"Do you think he can tell that you are a male and I'm a female?"

"No," I don't believe so, but I could be wrong.

You know, sometimes, you talk in a circle. I start talking about the same thing over and over again. The small alien now started approaching them. Linnet sighted it as it was coming. Oh no, Gary, the alien's walking around to us.

"What should we do?"

"Just let him be"

I don't think he can talk like we can; he might communicate another way; perhaps he communicates through teleplay.

Yeah, that could be true. Look at the alien he keeps staring at me; it's like he knows that we are talking to each other.

I think the alien's mad at us; suddenly, the alien began to stretch out his left arm. His little fingers kept on moving, and his eyes seemed to be moving as well.

"Why don't you put your hand in his hand and see what he does?"

"I don't think that's an excellent idea, Linnet."

"What if he takes my hand and breaks it?"

"He won't harm you"

You don't know that. You're making me take all the risks, and I wouldn't say I like it. Alright, then I will put my hand in his hand.

Linnet ever so slowly approached the alien and placed her hand in the Palm of the alien's right hand. The alien's body began to vibrate, and their Palm of his began to heat up. Linnet looked surprised; she couldn't understand what was happening to the alien.

I don't know what just happened, but the alien's Palm is beginning to heat up; it's like there's a heater inside of his hand. His whole hand is vibrating like the rest of his body is.

"What do the vibrations feel like?"

"It's hard for me to tell."

I feel like I'm getting lightheaded, and I might collapse. I keep finding myself staring into the eyes of the alien. It's like my eyes want to keep staring—all of a sudden, blue light of energy formed in the alien's left hand.

The blue light was so bright that it burned Linnet's eyes. The alien kneeled and felt Linnet's left leg. Hey Gary, this alien is beginning to freak me out.

This alien's studying me, and I wouldn't say I like it. I don't think the alien understands why we are here. The alien turned his back towards Linnet.

Gary, I don't understand why the alien just turned his back to us. Maybe he's tired of looking at us; no, I don't think so, I think he's trying to make some bomb and doesn't want us to see it.

I hope you are wrong. I'm scared enough right now. Then suddenly, the alien turned back around and faced Linnet.

Look, you, silly alien

   "Are you going to talk to me or what?"

   "The alien never even said a word."

He had his arms crossed and had a puzzled look on his face.

"Did you look at the alien's feet yet?"

"No," I just noticed that alien has five toes as we do.

You're so observant. This alien will go back to him and tell his folks that he met some crazy people who wouldn't stop staring at him. I don't think the alien has a sense of humor; he seems like he's always serious.

Aliens aren't like us at all; I beg to differ with that. I'm talking about the alien's brain; the alien probably has a much smaller brain than we do. I don't think so.

I believe that we have done enough talking; I don't think so, I want to stay here and see what the alien will do. Listen, I'm tired of standing and must find a place to sit down before falling.

"Why don't you sit on that large Boulder over there?"

"That would be too hard for me to sit on. It would make my hips ache."

"Do you realize that you're talking like an older man?"

"Yes," I do

"Do you have a problem with that?"

"No," hey look

Look at those strange floating clouds. I've never seen clouds so low to the ground. I wonder what kind of clouds they are. Stop worrying about everything else besides the alien. The alien is probably running out of patients with us and would like us to leave him alone.

"Mr. alien, could you please open your mouth for me?"

"There was dead silence once again."

"Would you please stop trying to talk to the alien?"

"No," I don't want to stop

I will stop talking to him when I'm ready. He's my friend, and he won't hurt me. That's what you think. He is like a wild animal. You don't know what he is going to do.

His whole body is glowing blue. I wonder why this is happening. Maybe you finally got on his nerves; oh, don't say that, Gary. If I were him, I would run away from you, Linnet. Of course, you would, but you are no alien, so you wouldn't understand how this alien must feel.

The one white cloud is floating over here; I want to touch it and see what happens. I wouldn't feel the cloud;

> "What if you get a shock from it?"

> "No," that won't occur; clouds don't shock you.

> "So now you are the expert on clouds?"

> "No," I didn't say I was.

We all know how clouds on Earth are on, but you and I don't see how the clouds are on another planet.

That's true, so I better be careful, I guess. I should have just let you touch the cloud, but I didn't want to see you get hurt anyway. That's nice of you, you are an alright man after all. The alien must of grew tired of standing and sat down on the dusty ground.

"Why are you still standing?"

"I thought you were going to sit down?"

I was, but I won't sit down until I find something soft to sit on.

Listen, Gary, you need to sit and not worry about sitting on something soft. but you don't have hips that are hurting you.

That's true, I'm used to standing for long periods, well that's great for you, but I can't stand up all day.

"Why's that?"

"I just get stiff then I get bad cramps in my calves."

You poor man, don't pity me, Linnet, just let it go. Someday you will get old and get cramps just like me. I tend to keep my body in good shape

"How about you?"

"Yeah, lousy health runs in my family."

I'm sorry to hear that. Gary was now looking impatient as they stayed close to the alien who wasn't saying anything to them. I think the alien should leave now. No, I don't think so, I'm not done checking him out.

"What else do you want to see?"

"I want to see how he breaths."

Gary was beginning to be worried about the too much attention Linnet was giving to the alien. He didn't see it to be necessary.

Why do you care about how he breaths?

"I'm just curious."

“Do you know how an alien breaths?”

“No,” I don't, and I don't care.

I have enough things to worry about with myself then figure out how an alien takes his next breath. You are just getting tired no, I'm not tired, I'm just getting a migraine.

“Is it me?”

“No,” it's not

My body, all of a sudden, feels like it is off balance.

“Why don't you look at the oxygen gauge on your right arm and see if your oxygen is going down?”

“The indicator says that my oxygen is at ninety-seven percent.”

“Are you still feeling so warm?”

“No,” I think just comfortable, and actually, it's getting cold out here.

Meanwhile, Lucas was making sure that the spacecraft was still in good shape. He got on his hands and knees and looked at the bottom of the craft. There was no sign of damage. He heard a loud rumble and looked behind him and saw a giant green lizard.

It startled him and made him fall back into the spacecraft. He couldn't understand what the giant lizard was all about. It looked scary, and it was his first time seeing a lizard that big. Gary and Linnet weren't with him.

They would have all figured out stuff about the lizard together. Lucas thought to himself, I have never seen such a giant lizard in my life. He quickly unlatched the door and jumped into the spacecraft.

He was shaking like a leaf. He thought to himself; I hope that the lizard goes away to get back to work. He looked out one of the windows and saw the lizard.

The lizard kept on slowly walking along. It seemed to Lucas like the lizard was just looking for something to eat.

The green lizard kept on sticking out his sizeable pink tongue, and his tail kept on swinging back and forth. Lucas thought I wish that I had some treat I could give to the lizard so that he would leave me alone.

Lucas forgot to tie down his tools, and a screwdriver and hammer began to float in midair just past his head. Since the gravity on the planet was not really there, everything that wasn't securely fashioned had come to lose and was floating around inside the spacecraft. Off to his left side was a floating bottle of water, Lucas's lips were parched, and his lips were turning all white.

I'm not feeling so well, he thought. His stomach was grumbling, and he had an eyelash fall into his right eye. He immediately took off his space helmet and took off his gloves. He reached up and got the eyelash out of his sight.

Chapter Seven: Help

His right vision was blurry afterward, and he found a small mirror and looked into him himself. He noticed that his eye was turning red and becoming glazed over, then the pain came.

His right eye was hurting so much that he had close it for a couple of minutes. Ouch, my eye hurts so bad. Since he still had one of his eyes open, he looked out the window again and saw that giant green lizard was gone.

He didn't know where the lizard had gone, and he was too focused on his eyes that he didn't notice when the lizard was leaving.

Lucas came to the realization that; he might not be able to open his right eye again. He looked back in the mirror, and his right eye was getting all puffy, and it hurt to the touch. He knew that he better do something about it and soon.

He didn't want to risk losing his right eye. The thought of losing his good sight on the mission looked too depressing; he would do his best so that that wouldn't happen to him.

He floated to the back of the spacecraft and saw that the first aid kit was missing, which drove him crazy. He floated all around in the spaceship, and still, he could not find the first aid kit.

The back of the spaceship was dark, and there wasn't much light coming in from the window. He opened a drawer, and everything in the drawer floated up and remained out of reach; he reached up and grabbed the items back.

There was a pair of scissors and a notebook. A pair of sunglasses floated on past him, and he couldn't reach them to put them back away; this made him frustrated and irritable.

He was working up a sweat just from floating around and trying to reach out and grab all the stuff that came out of the drawer. It took him five minutes just to get everything back in the drawer.

There was a second drawer right below that one. He didn't dare to open that one; he was too scared that there might be tools in there. Opening them would mean them rushing at him, and he could get stabbed in the process.

There was a small lock on the drawer anyway, so it must have been locked. He found a switch and flicked it on. He didn't see anything happen.

He flicked it on and off one more time and realized that the button had turned on the outside lights. He turned them off, and then he saw another button, he hit this switch, and the interior lights turned on.

He was glad to see the light. Now that he could see better, he got back to looking for the first aid kit. He knew that the first aid kit had to be nearby. He went to the front of the spacecraft and saw that one of the cabinets off to his left hand had been left open, and he was not sure why it was left open.

He floated over to it and saw a plastic bucket and a pair of tweezers in the bucket. There was a label on the side of the bucket; it read, place any soil samples inside of the bucket, then seals it up. Lucas thought, okay, so I guess I will be the one going to collect the soil sample.

His right eye kept pulsating in pain; it was like the nerve in his right eye wasn't correct. Now his right eye was beginning to itch. He could barely stand it anymore. Now he was becoming more irritated, so he took a deep breath, trying to relax. The inside of the spacecraft was hot, almost like a sauna.

The sweat began to pour down his eyebrows. He wiped away the work with his left hand and made sure that no work could go into his eyes. There was a small cabinet by one of the main control panels. He thought to himself, this better be where the first aid kit is, or I will go out of my mind.

He tried to open it, but it seemed to be jammed shut. He grabbed onto the gray handle and pulled as hard as he could. Something released, and Lucas went floating back into the window.

He swam back over to the drawer, and there was the first aid kit. A great sigh of relief came over him. He thought to himself, thank goodness I found it.

Now everything is going to be better. He took out the first aid kit and tried to open it, but it was all taped shut. The first aid kit was a metal tin.

It had a white cross on the front of it. He tried to get the tape off, but it proved to be too difficult. So he took the kit along with him to where the scissors were.

He opened the drawer that had the scissors in it, and the scissors floated out, and the sharp tips of the scissors got stock in his spacesuit.

The scissors had damaged his suit pretty severely. So badly that he realized that he wouldn't be able to go outside of the spacecraft.

Now he would have to stay trapped in the spacecraft until Linnet and Gary got back. He thought to himself, at least I'm still alive and well. Once he had a hold of the scissors, he began to get the first aid kit open.

The sharp scissors cut right through the thick tape. He popped open the kit and was pleased to see everything he needed to fix up his eye. Then suddenly, the ground shook beneath the spacecraft.

The spacecraft now had fallen off of its secure stand and was no longer stable and began to roll down the slight incline that was right next to it.

The spacecraft rolled into a pile of huge boulders, and on the other side of the boulders was a sheer drop-off. Linnet and Gary were getting closer to their spacecraft.

They were a few yards away from it, I'm getting tired of walking; hang in there; he's now back at our spacecraft. By the way, I've heard that we may come in contact with reptilian humanoids.

"Who told you that?"

"A professor that I also know now works for the international space station."

I hope Lucas is doing okay; I'm sure he's doing just fine, Linnet. Hey, look, I see Lucas.

"What's he doing in there?"

"It seems to me that he's floating around in the spacecraft."

"Does he look like he is awake?"

"No," I believe that he is sleeping.

Alright, then, I'm going to check on him. Gary and Linnet opened the pressure-sealed door and entered the spacecraft. They took off their spacesuits and looked at Lucas.

"Can you hear us?"

"There was still no answer."

I think there's something wrong with Lucas.

"How do you know?"

"He won't even talk or listen to me."

Just give him some time, and he might listen to you.

"What's that crawling along the floor of the spacecraft?"

"I don't know, and I didn't see what you were talking about."

"What exactly did it look like?"

"It looked like a gecko Linnet but every movement I do, it does the same."

I'm more worried about Lucas than some silly Gecko creature. Let's take care of Lucas, then we can chase after that juvenile gecko. The Gecko just jumped on my shoulder, Just let him go; I'm working on Lucas.

"Can't you see I'm busy"

"Please wake up"

I don't think what you are trying to do is
working, Linnet.

"How do you know?"

"You are no Dr, so maybe I have my own
opinions."

I think that Lucas is dead, okay then he's dead.

"What are we going to do now?"

"I'm not sure what to do next."

We should get barely him on this planet.

"Are you out of your mind?"

"No," he needs a proper burial place.

You're a crazy man thank you for the comment.

"What about this gecko you saw?"

"He's still on my left shoulder; don't you
see him?"

I do see him, and every movement you or I do, he
does. He's a great mimicker, and I think we

should take him home with us. I would like to keep him as a pet; I don't think WASA would allow that.

"How are we going to get back to earth?"

"Why are you asking me that?"

"Because I'm looking out the side window, I noticed that the side thruster is badly damaged"

We won't be able to get us back into the atmosphere. Hold on, let me call WASA; it will just take a moment. He dialed the number, and there was no reply, Linnet I just dialed the number, and there was no reply. I think that I discovered what killed Lucas, there was a small hole in the back of his spacesuit, and he couldn't get enough oxygen; it's known as a silent killer. This mission was doomed from the beginning.

Let's just open up this spacecraft and let the outside air come in and kill us; no I won't let you do that; suddenly a flaming star came flying along and struck the spacecraft and had enough force to throw the spacecraft off the side of the cliff.

The spacecraft fell one hundred feet and killed Linnet and Gary instantly when it hit bottom. A week later WASA, sent out a rescue team. They searched high and low, and even searched on three different planets and weren't able to find their bodies or the spacecraft.